SAM SILVER: UNDERCOVER PIRATE

Collect all the Sam Silver: Undercover Pirate *books*

DRAGON FIRE

Jan Burchett and Sara Vogler

Illustrated by Leo Hartas

Orion
Children's Books

First published in Great Britain in 2013
by Orion Children's Books
a division of the Orion Publishing Group Ltd
Orion House
5 Upper St Martin's Lane
London WC2H 9EA
An Hachette UK company

1 3 5 7 9 10 8 6 4 2

A catalogue record for this book is available from the British Library.

ISBN 978 1 4440 0588 2

Printed in Great Britain by Clays Ltd, St Ives plc

For Jeremiah and Trey.
Keep up the reading! Love, Jan and Sara

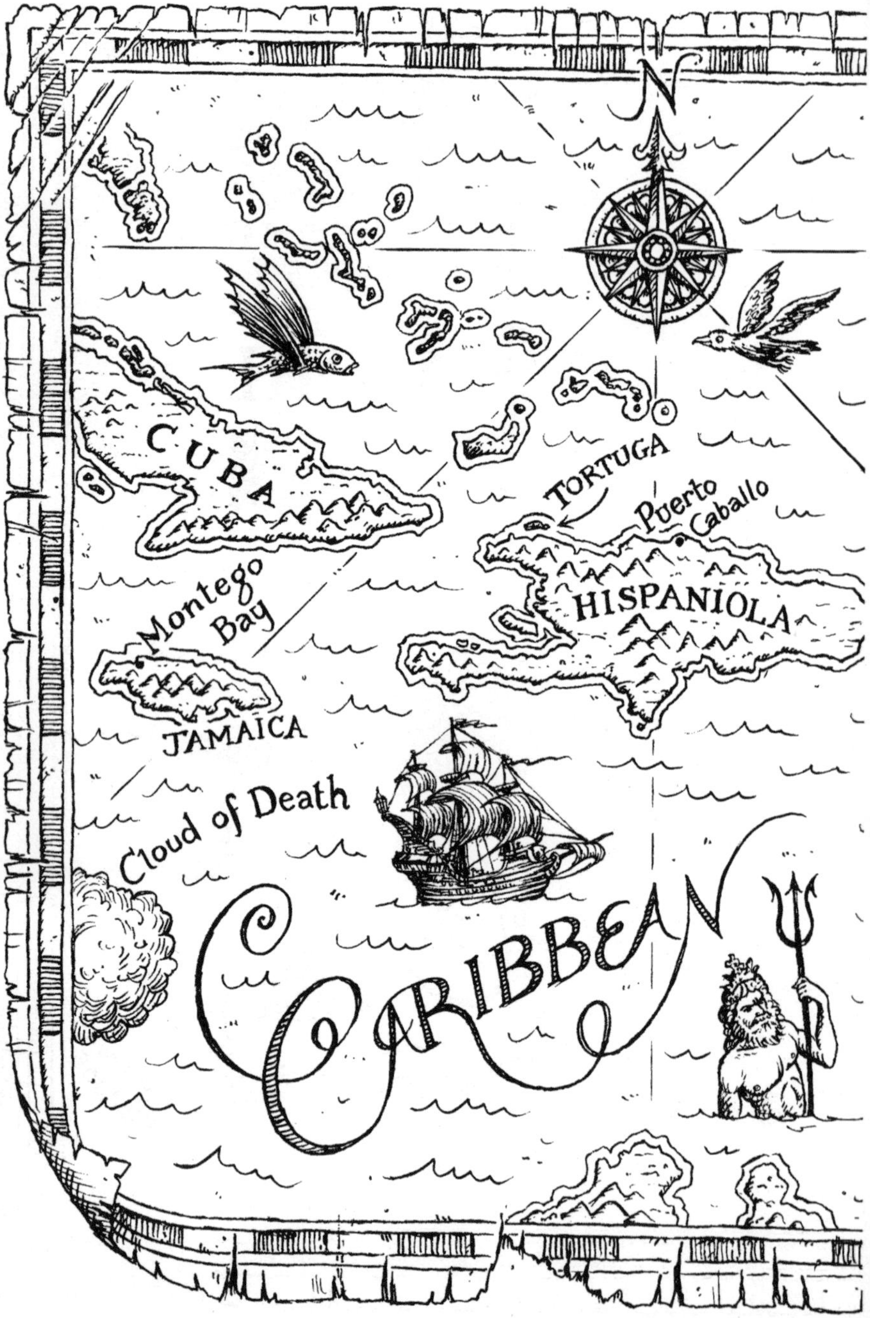

CUBA

Montego
Bay

JAMAICA

Cloud of Death

TORTUGA

Puerto
Caballo

HISPANIOLA

CARIBBEAN

The SEA WOLF

Captain's Cabin
Hammocks
Gun Deck
Galley
Ship's Stores

CHAPTER ONE

Sam Silver opened his eyes and jumped out of bed. It was Saturday and Saturday meant a fantastic game of football down on the beach with his mates. But he could hear a spattering sound against his bedroom window. He pulled the curtains and groaned – rain was coming down in sheets! The high street was deserted and he could hardly

see the sand of Backwater Bay in the grey
mist. His heart sank to the bottom of his
pyjamas. There'd be no football this
morning.

He glanced over at the shelf on his
bedroom wall. It was covered in things he'd
found washed up by the sea. In the middle
stood the old sand-pitted bottle that was
more valuable to him than the World Cup!

Inside lay a gold doubloon, put there three hundred years ago by his pirate ancestor, Joseph Silver. The coin had the power to take him back in time to the *Sea Wolf*, a real pirate ship.

"Well, if I can't play footie," he said to the bottle, "I'll have an adventure instead – in the hot Caribbean sunshine."

Sam knew no one would miss him. No time ever passed in the present when he was back in 1706. He quickly dressed in the scruffy jeans and T-shirt that he always wore when he took up his buccaneer duties. He tipped the coin out of the bottle, spat on it and rubbed it on his sleeve.

Sam's bedroom walls began to spin. He caught a glimpse of his rain-soaked window rushing by before he was lifted into the dark tunnel of time and whooshed around. It was like being inside a monster vacuum cleaner. The next instant he found himself sitting on the floor of the storeroom of the *Sea Wolf*. But the ship was tipping violently from side to side. He was flung against a barrel then thrown onto a coil of rope. The ship's timbers creaked and groaned as if they were going to break.

"Batten down the hatches!" came a squawk and the ship's parrot flew out from behind a chest and landed on his shoulder.

"Hello there, Crow," said Sam, delighted to see his feathery friend. "What's happening? Let's get up on deck and see."

He spotted his belt, spyglass and jerkin scattered across the floor. His friend Charlie had left them for him, as she always did when Sam was whisked home to the future. The bold girl pirate was the only one on board who knew his time-travelling secret. He was pleased to see that she'd found him a new neckerchief too — he'd blown the last one up. Sam put on his pirate gear and grabbed hold of the door handle. The tossing motion of the ship flung him against the door, but with the next roll, he forced it open and burst out. He staggered up the steps to the main deck.

There was no sign of the sparkling sea and blue Caribbean sky that he usually saw when he arrived in the past. Fierce black clouds raced overhead and waves crashed against the sides of the ship. Rain hammered the deck, drenching him instantly. Through the downpour he could see the captain struggling to keep the wheel steady.

Harry Hopp, a stocky pirate with a wooden leg, was hauling on a rope. "Someone help me get these sails round," he yelled.

With Crow clinging to his shoulder, Sam lurched across the streaming deck. He joined the first mate and seized the end of the rope.

"I'll help, Mr Hopp," he bellowed over the wind, pulling with all his strength.

"Stap me!" cried Harry, his stubbly face breaking into a broad grin. "It's Sam Silver! How did you get here in this storm?"

Sam didn't know what to say. "Er . . . I . . . well . . ." he spluttered. Charlie usually got him out of this sort of pickle, but she was nowhere to be seen. Then it came to him. "I got here before the storm started!"

"I never saw you," shouted Harry.

"Never saw you," the parrot repeated helpfully.

"Of course not," panted Sam as he worked. "That's because, er . . . I was just coming up on deck when the storm began. Yes, that's it, and I got thrown about and bumped my head and . . ."

Two huge hands took hold of the rope behind him.

"Well, boil me up for breakfast!" It was

Ned the cheerful bosun. "The poor boy must have knocked himself out! And yet here he is, getting to work straight away."

"Aye," said Harry, lashing the rope to a strong wooden hook. "He's a true Silver, just like his grandfather, God rest his soul."

The pirates thought that Sam was Joseph Silver's grandson. Sam went along with this. He couldn't tell them just how many "greats" there really were in between.

"We're glad you're back!" called Captain Blade from the wheel. The weapons in the belts across his chest glistened with rain, and his dark hair and beard hung in rats' tails.

Sam battled through the wind to reach him.

"Keep your distance," ordered the captain, eyeing Crow who was still on Sam's shoulder. Captain Blade was the bravest man Sam knew, but the sight of the green bird always made him go pale. Peter the cook claimed it was because a parrot had pooed on him in his pram, but every pirate on the *Sea Wolf* had a different story about the reason for the captain's one fear. However, they all agreed about one thing – when Captain Blade was around, the parrot was to be called a Caribbean crow. That way the captain could pretend he had nothing to be scared of.

Blade looked up at the sky. "By Orion, I think the storm's abating ahead," he said. "Those clouds don't look as heavy and I'd bet a bag of doubloons that the waves aren't as high."

"We'll soon be back on course," agreed Harry Hopp.

"Where were you heading?" asked Sam.

"Till this weather came along, we were

following a French treasure fleet," the captain told him.

"They'll be scattered in the storm by now," said Harry Hopp with a cunning grin. "Easier to make one of them a target."

Great! thought Sam. *A treasure hunt.*

"Set sail north-east," ordered the captain. "There's nothing can stop us now."

Someone came pounding up the steps from the gun deck below. One look at the long curly hair and bright bandana and Sam knew it was his friend Fernando.

He ran across to greet him, but Fernando was making straight for Captain Blade. He was muttering under his breath in Spanish.

"We're leaking, Captain!" he cried. "And it's bad!"

CHAPTER TWO

"Where's the leak?" demanded Ned.

"Well below the waterline," Fernando reported. "Starboard bow."

Ned called to some men and took them down to inspect the damage.

Fernando suddenly spotted Sam and for a moment his worried face broke into a grin. "Good to see you, my friend!" He slapped Sam on the back. "Wait a minute, how did you get here in this raging storm?"

Sam quickly repeated his tale about how he'd arrived before the storm but then bumped his head.

"Maybe it'll knock some sense into you," came a voice. "Lord knows you could do with it!" It was Charlie, staggering across the swaying deck, her pirate clothes soaked and dripping. The ship's cat dangled in her arms. Sinbad looked very bedraggled and even more surly than usual.

"Drowned rat!" squawked Crow, eyeing him beadily.

With an angry hiss, Sinbad swiped a claw at the parrot. Crow screeched and flapped up to the top of the mainmast.

"Naughty kitty," said Charlie fondly, tickling him on his tummy. The black cat purred and nuzzled Charlie's arm. She was the only one of the crew who could get within a paw's reach of him.

Ned came running back. "We're shipping an ocean of water, Captain," he said. "I've got men on the pumps and we're trying to plug it."

"Can it be repaired?" asked Blade.

"Not at sea," replied Ned. "We need to get at it from the outside. There's only one thing for it. We'll have to careen the ship."

The captain looked up at the sky, where the black clouds were breaking up with blue patches between. "Now the worst of the storm's passed we can find land."

"What does careen mean?" asked Sam. "And why do we need land to do it?"

"We beach the ship," the captain explained. "Then, when it's out of the water, we can get to the damage."

"I saw that once in a film!" gasped Sam. "Except it was a spaceship and— Ouch!"

Charlie had kicked him in the shin. He realised Ned and Captain Blade were gawping at him. He was always forgetting that things in 1706 were very different from the twenty-first century.

"*Space*ship?" said Ned. "What's the boy talking about?"

"Don't worry." Charlie laughed. "Bumping his head has made him even more daft than usual!"

"Silly me," said Sam. "I meant that there'll be lots of space for the ship on the beach."

Ned chuckled. "You're a strange one, Sam Silver."

"The pumps aren't coping, Captain," came a bellow from the gun deck.

"Start bailing!" Blade shouted back.

Charlie and Fernando grabbed buckets and ran to help empty the water out of the hold. Sam headed after them.

"No, you come with me, lad," cried the captain, taking the steps to the foredeck in two bounds. "I need your keen eyes to find the nearest land. You take the port side."

A shaft of sunlight burst through the clouds, cutting through the drizzle and lighting up the grey sea. The choppy waves slapped at the bows as the *Sea Wolf* ploughed through the water.

Sam swept the horizon with his spyglass. "Nothing this side, Captain," he reported.

"And nothing to starboard either," muttered Captain Blade. "We'd better find land soon or we'll be in trouble."

The empty sea stretched ahead. But then a tiny speck appeared on the horizon. Sam adjusted his spyglass and peered intently at

it. Gradually a
small mound
of green came
into view.

"Land ho!"
he cried.

"You're right,
lad," said Captain
Blade, coming to
join him. "Island, eleven o'clock!" he
called down to Harry Hopp.

The first mate ran to the wheel and
turned it to change course. "Pull on those
sheets!" he barked. "We'll need all the sail
we can muster."

The crew hauled on the ropes to pull
the sails into the right position.

"Let's hope the wind gets us there
before the sea sinks us," muttered Blade
grimly. "The land can't come soon
enough."

The *Sea Wolf* was making heavy weather

against the waves. The water was still rough although the storm clouds were way off in the distance now.

Sam trained his spyglass on the island. He could make out a forested mountain, grey clouds swirling round its flattened peak. He turned to tell the captain. Blade was gazing out at the approaching land, a deep frown on his forehead.

"What's the matter, Captain?" asked Sam.

Blade pulled at the red braids in his beard. "I've heard whispers about this place in many a sailor's tale." He led the way down to the main deck, where some of the crew were staring at the island, pointing and muttering to each other.

"'Tis just as they say," said Harry Hopp, a troubled look on his face. "The flat-topped mountain that seems to make its own clouds."

"Some said it didn't exist," added Ben

Hudson, wiping his forehead with his bandana.

"We *hoped* it didn't," muttered Harry under his breath.

"Why?" asked Sam. He felt a thrill of fear rush through him. "Where are we?"

Captain Blade slapped his spyglass on the palm of his hand. "Dragon Island."

CHAPTER THREE

"Dragon Island!" gasped Sam. "Is there a real dragon there?"

"Aye, so they say," growled Harry Hopp. "Though no one's seen it in living memory."

Awesome! thought Sam. He hoped it was true. He knew there weren't any dragons in his day, but perhaps that was only because they'd died out by the twenty-first century.

After all, there were lots of *ancient* stories about them. Maybe three hundred years ago they really had roamed the world, breathing fire and flying about frightening people.

"'Tis said that the fire and smoke from the dragon can be seen from miles away," Harry went on as they sailed into a calm bay with a long golden beach. "My grandfather would have it that when he was a boy, a Spanish ship disappeared and only its burnt figurehead was ever found. Everyone said it was the beast that did for it."

Sam looked at the deserted sands and the slopes of the mountain that rose above.

"What about the people who live here though?" he persisted. "Surely they know all about it."

"I doubt that there's any folk living on this forsaken isle," said Ben. "They'd have been dragon dinner long since."

The bailing crew came up on deck. As

each man spotted the island, he stopped in his tracks and stared, aghast. Everyone seemed to have heard of the dreaded place.

Charlie was last to appear. "Dragon Island!" she cried, dropping her bucket in shock.

"By Neptune, we'll be away from here before the dragon shows its ugly face," Captain Blade assured the pirates. "Make ready for beaching!"

"Aye, aye, Captain," said Harry Hopp. "Ben, get the strongest ropes we have. The rest of you, get your muscles ready. We've a ship to pull onto the sand."

"Hold hard!" came a shout from the bow. "Keel about to strike."

A shudder ran through the *Sea Wolf* as she hit the bottom and slowly began to tilt.

"Shipwreck!" shrieked Crow.

Sam stood on the beach, gazing at the *Sea Wolf*. She lay on her side, a gaping hole on her green, barnacled hull, looking like a wounded beast. She reminded him of the pictures on the news when whales got stranded and lay helpless on the sand.

The bosun set about ordering men to cut down trees for timber and Harry and the captain climbed onto the hull to look at the damage.

Fernando swung up to join them, fell to his knees and pulled his knife out of his belt.

"What are you doing?" called Sam.

"Scraping the barnacles off while I've got the chance," Fernando called back. "They stick to the bottom of the ship and after a while, they really slow her down. When the repair is finished, we'll turn her over and do the other side."

"Can I help?" Sam asked. "I'm sure I'll be a brilliant barnacle remover."

Fernando laughed and shook his head.

"It's a skilled job – too skilled for you. You'd probably make more holes! Here, you can be the barnacle catcher." He threw a weed-encrusted shell down to Sam.

Peter the cook scuttled over with a bucket and eagerly scooped up the shells that Sam was collecting. "These will make a tasty stew," he told him.

Oh, dear, thought Sam, remembering some of the meals that Peter had prepared. *It would only be tasty if you liked chewing through cardboard and old socks.*

Peter rattled his bucket. "Now I just need some onions and—" He broke off and a look of fear came over his face as he stared at the mountain. "We've woken the dragon!" he wailed. "I can see its breath."

Sam followed his gaze up the forested hill, his heart thumping.

Wisps of smoke rose from the flat peak. Sam could imagine they'd been puffed out of a giant mouth.

He felt tingles of nervous excitement run through him at the thought of a huge scaly monster roaming the island. "Maybe there *is* a dragon here," he muttered to himself. He was determined to find out!

CHAPTER FOUR

"Sam Silver!" called Ben. "Stop gawping at the skies and come here. I've got a job for you."

Sam snapped out of his daydream. Charlie was at his side, an empty sack slung over her shoulder and bottles in her hands.

"Ben wants us to find food and water," she told him, handing over the bottles.

"There'll be plenty of fruit in the trees nearby, and there's a stream running down to the beach not far away."

The two friends marched off into the forest. When they'd got all their provisions, Sam pulled at Charlie's arm, a mischievous glint in his eye.

"How about we explore the mountain while we've got the chance?" he suggested.

Charlie's eyes grew wide. "What about the dragon?"

"If we're really quiet we won't disturb it," Sam assured her.

"So you're a dragon expert!" laughed Charlie. "Are there lots of them around in your time?"

"Never seen one," said Sam. "But I'd like to – wouldn't you?"

"It would be amazing." Charlie grinned. "Or 'awesome' as you would say."

"Let's do it then!" declared Sam, putting his bottles down. "We'll leave everything here so we can be quick, otherwise the rest of the crew will wonder where we've gone."

He led the way between the trees. As they crunched through thick, tangled undergrowth that grew between the stout trunks, Sam suddenly felt a strange sensation, as if he was being watched. He'd felt like this before on board ship. Usually it was the baleful eyes of the ship's cat.

"Is Sinbad around?" he asked Charlie as he pulled a creeper out of his way.

"No, I left him asleep in a coil of rope," said Charlie. "Why?"

"Nothing," replied Sam, with a shiver. He shook himself. Of course he wasn't being watched. He'd just been thinking about dragons too much!

Soon they were steadily climbing the slope of the mountain, pushing aside creepers and brambles to make a rough pathway. The forest came to an abrupt end and the peak stood out against the bright sky. Smoke – or was it dragon's breath? – rose in sudden gusts, then gathered and hung over the mountain in a grey cloud.

There were bushes here and there but gradually the ground became bare and stony. The only sign of life was the occasional insect buzzing by. Sam sped up. He couldn't wait to get to the top. He might be about to see a real live dragon!

"Slow down!" panted Charlie, slipping and sliding on the loose stones. "It's all right for you in those funny shoes," she pointed to his trainers, "but I have bare feet, remember."

Sam took her hand and together they picked their way over the hard, cindery ground.

At last the peak was in reach.

His stomach bubbling with excitement, Sam clawed his way up the last of the slope towards the top, helping Charlie up after him. Charlie suddenly pulled back.

"Come on!" urged Sam. "Not far now."

Charlie frowned. "I know you're eager to see this dragon," she said in a low voice, "but we don't want *it* to see *us.*"

"Good point," admitted Sam.

They set off again, moving more slowly now, trying not to dislodge the loose stones under their hands and feet. At last they were at the rim.

"Ready?" whispered Sam.

Charlie nodded.

Very carefully they drew themselves up and peeped over together.

They stared in surprise at the grey crater that lay below them.

"It's like a giant bowl!" whispered Charlie. "The dragon must be underneath – look at the smoke coming through those cracks."

Sam shook his head, trying not to feel too disappointed. Of course there was no dragon. There couldn't be. Dragons belonged in story books. But something was going on in this deep crater – and now Sam knew exactly what it was. He'd seen television programmes about mountains with flat-topped peaks and smoke rising from deep craters. "There's no dragon here," he said slowly. "This is a volcano!"

Charlie looked at him, puzzled. "A vol-cay-no?" she repeated. "What's that?"

"It's a special type of mountain," Sam explained. "Inside there's rock that's so hot it's turned to liquid. Sometimes it gets too hot and the top sort of explodes with flames and smoke. Then all the molten rock comes pouring down the outside. That's called 'an eruption' and it destroys everything in its path."

Charlie stared at him. "Are you pulling my leg?" she demanded.

"No," said Sam. "It's true."

"No wonder passing sailors thought there was a dragon if they saw that," said Charlie. "Is this mountain going to explode?"

"Looks like it," said Sam, grimly. "And very soon."

Charlie's eyes grew wide with alarm. "Then we must all get off the island as soon as we can!" she said, backing away from the rim.

"Too right," agreed Sam, heading off

down the slope. "We'll have to tell the crew that the dragon has woken up. It'll be easier than trying to explain what a volcano is."

Slipping and sliding on the cindery rubble, they made their way quickly down the mountainside. When they reached the trees, they grabbed their bags and ran for the beach.

"Did you get lost?" asked Harry Hopp, wiping his forehead on his sleeve. "We're nearly dead from lack of fresh food!"

"Sorry," said Sam. "But we found out something important ..."

"There can't be anything more important than what's in those bags of yours," Ben interrupted. "I'm starving."

Sam and Charlie handed out the bananas, berries and nuts they'd found.

"Captain Blade," Charlie began. "We think the drag—"

"Don't mention that creature by name!"

hissed Ned nervously. "It might think we're calling it."

Peter the cook chewed as he stirred his cauldron over an open fire. "This fruit stuff's all very well for parrots," he said, "but you wait till you get my barnacle stew inside you. Just needs a few more hours."

"I hope we'll have sailed before that," muttered Ben.

"Aye," whispered Ned. "We can leave the stew for the . . . beast!"

"Back to work now, men," ordered Captain Blade as soon as the food had gone. "The repairs are nowhere near finished yet."

The crew began to mutter and cast nervous glances at the mountain top, where the clouds were growing thicker by the minute.

"I don't like this place," said Peter gloomily. "We've wakened that monster, no doubt about it."

"We've made enough racket to wake the dead," agreed Fernando.

Ned shrugged. "What choice did we have? You can't repair a ship silently!"

"Isn't she sound enough to sail a little way, Captain?" asked Ben. "To another island, maybe? We should be gone from this one, that's for sure." He looked up again at the mountain. "I don't want to meet any flying lizards."

Anxious muttering spread round the crew.

That's it, thought Sam. *I don't need to tell them anything about the volcano. The crew are so scared of the dragon we'll be off any minute.*

The captain jumped to his feet, a look of anger on his face. "Avast your whingeing!" he bellowed. "Anyone who wants to leave now will have to swim, and good luck to 'em."

"That's right," said Harry. "Dragon or no dragon, the rest of us will leave when the *Sea Wolf*'s good and ready. That hole is too bad to take to sea. The only place we'll go is straight to Davy Jones' Locker if we sail now."

"Keep the noise down and the dragon will go back to sleep," said Blade. "He'll give us no trouble, I'll be bound. Back to work, I say!"

"But, Captain," Sam burst out. He realised that everyone was staring at him, but even if they thought he'd gone crazy, he had to tell them the truth. "It won't make any difference how noisy we are. It's not what you think in that mountain, it's a volcano! And it might erupt at any time!"

CHAPTER FIVE

"What mad talk is this, Sam Silver?" demanded Captain Blade.

Charlie leapt to Sam's rescue. "He means it's a special sort of dragon," she said quickly.

Sam nodded vigorously. "It's called a volcano dragon. And if it erupts that means ... er ..."

"... that means it gets very angry," said Charlie.

"Which it could do at any moment," Sam finished.

There was a horrified silence.

"How do you know all this?" asked Fernando at last.

"My mum told me about volcano dragons," said Sam. "She's a bit of an expert. She said they puff smoke and puke really hot stuff that bubbles down the mountain and fries you in seconds."

Captain Blade stood up. "Well, if we've got a volcano dragon on our hands, we have all the more reason to get those repairs finished in double quick time. To work, men!"

"Thanks, Charlie," Sam whispered to his friend. "You got me out of that one."

Charlie grinned. "As usual," she whispered back. "I just wish we could leave now."

Soon the air was filled with the sound of hasty sawing and hammering. The light was beginning to fade and lanterns were lit and hung from branches stuck into the sand. Peter stirred his stew, sending wafts of foul-smelling steam into the air.

Sam had the strange feeling that he was being watched again. He whirled round but there was nothing there. He suddenly noticed that the lanterns had begun to swing on their posts. *That's odd*, he thought. *There's no breeze.* Now he could feel a slight tremor under his feet. The other pirates felt it too. They put down their tools. There was dead silence for a moment, then a fierce shudder shook the ground, rattling the *Sea Wolf* from bows to stern. The lanterns swung wildly as a deep rumble filled the air.

The crew looked fearfully up at the mountain. Steam was spurting from its peak in great gusts.

"The volcano dragon!" cried Peter, dropping his ladle. "It's coming!"

The ground shook again. The pirates ran around the beached ship, frantically searching the sky and all yelling at once.

"Help! It's going to see us!"

"Let's get out of here."

"Where can we hide?"

Captain Blade leapt up on to the *Sea Wolf* hull. "Are we men or mice?" he demanded fiercely. "We don't shy away from danger like lily-livered slime worms."

"But, Captain," called Ben, nervously, "what can we do if the dragon decides to come down from its lair and eat us?"

"If we meet the volcano dragon we shall fight it like true pirates!" declared Blade.

"That we will!" said Harry Hopp firmly. He picked up his hammer. "I'll swap this for a sword the moment that beast dares to come anywhere near! Now, let's get the ship seaworthy."

Heartened, the crew gave a cheer and turned to get on with their work.

Captain Blade beckoned to Sam and Charlie. "The crew look thirsty. Take Fernando and find some coconuts. The milk will do them good after all this work." He looked at the mountain, dark against the setting sun. "Ned, Ben," he called. "You go with them – just in case the dragon makes an appearance – and don't go too far!"

"Ahoy, shipmates!" came a squawk and Crow landed on Sam's head.

"And take that ... bird with you."

Ned and Ben grabbed lanterns and they all set off into the forest. Sam felt nervous. Was the volcano about to erupt? It seemed to have gone quiet for the moment. Maybe they'd get the ship repaired and away before it rumbled again.

Sam, Charlie and Fernando followed Ned and Ben's bobbing lanterns. They were glowing brightly now that the sun had set.

"Here's a good crop," called Fernando,

standing beside a tree that was bending under the weight of ripe coconuts. "Come and help me, Charlie."

A twig cracked somewhere in the forest. Sam froze. He had the strange prickling sensation at his back again. He was sure he was being watched. If he turned now, would there be two scaly eyes staring into his?

He was about to call to the others when there was a terrifying crashing in the undergrowth and a band of men burst out from the trees, brandishing clubs and spears. The pirates were surrounded.

CHAPTER SIX

The men made a silent circle around the five shipmates, spears pointed straight at their hearts. Their captors wore strange leggings made of animal hide and their arms and chests were covered in body paint. Sam's insides quivered. Every picture on their skin showed fire-breathing dragons with vicious claws and fearsome teeth.

"Enemy to starboard!" muttered Crow, hiding his beak in Sam's hair.

One of the warriors banged the ground with his spear. He wore a headdress of animal bones which made him tower over the others. "Not from our island," he cried in a strange accent.

This must be their leader, thought Sam. *And he speaks English!*

"Didn't think anyone lived here," muttered Ned out of the corner of his mouth. "Who are they?"

"Whoever they are, they don't like visitors," murmured Charlie, her eyes wide and staring.

"We could be in trouble here," whispered Ben nervously. "What would the captain do?"

Ned slowly put down his lantern and held out his hands, palms upwards, to show that they were empty. "We mean no harm," he said. "We just want to mend our ship and we'll be off."

"Not from our island," repeated the leader, jabbing his spear at Ned to force him back. "Dragon Wakers!"

"They think we woke the volcano dragon," hissed Fernando. "We're in trouble. Let's shout for help."

But as soon as he opened his mouth to yell, the leader pressed a spear up against his throat.

"Tongue still!" he hissed.

The islanders snatched away the pirates' weapons and forced them to walk through the trees, away from the sea and their friends, towards the foot of the volcano. The warriors barely spoke to each other but when they did, they used a strange-sounding language that Sam had never heard before. He could tell that none of the pirates understood it either.

"The captain won't know where we've gone," said Ben under his breath. He began to pull at his neckerchief. "I'll leave a trail to show him the way. Ow!" A sharp point jabbed him in the back. "No, I won't," he muttered ruefully.

The islanders marched the pirates up the slope of the mountain.

"Where are we going?" Charlie asked the

man who was striding along next to her. He was holding her roughly by the arm and making her stumble over the rough ground.

"And why are you taking us prisoner?" demanded Sam.

"Tongue still!" snapped one of their captors.

They halted in front of a large hole in the mountainside surrounded by a ring of boulders. One of the men picked up a long branch with sacking tied round the end. Sam saw a spark fly from a flint and the sacking flared into a flame, sending flickering beams over the grim faces of their captors. The torchbearer held the flame so that it lit up the hole. Now Sam could see a tunnel hacked out of the rock, leading away into the dark. One by one he and his companions were pushed along the tunnel, and made to follow the torch flame. Passages led off in different

directions where lights could be seen and
Sam could smell food cooking.

"Do you think they're taking us to their
homes?" whispered Charlie.

"Hope so," Sam whispered back. "The
cooking smells better than Peter's."

But the prisoners were marched onwards
until they reached a rough cave. The men
gave them a sharp push and they tumbled
down in a heap on the cold hard floor.

"Stay here!" ordered the leader, his face fierce and angry in the torchlight.

Their captors disappeared and the pirates were left in the pitch dark.

"Nighty night!" squawked Crow.

"I can't even see my hand in front of my face!" complained Ben.

"I have a candle stub," said Fernando. "Has anyone got a flint?"

"Can we risk it?" asked Sam. He lowered his voice. "I bet there are guards nearby who'll take it away. They'd have left us with a light if they'd wanted to."

"Good thinking," said Ben. "Let's save that candle."

The ground beneath them shuddered and they heard a distant rumble. *The volcano is still thinking about erupting*, thought Sam. *And now we're right inside it!*

"The volcano dragon sounds very angry," said Charlie quietly.

"I have a bad feeling about this!" came

Fernando's voice. "I believe our captors are going to punish us for disturbing it."

"I'm sure they'll let us go when they realise we didn't mean to," said Ned, though Sam could hear that even the bosun didn't sound his usual cheery self.

The slow beat of a drum began to echo eerily round the cave. Sam felt Charlie stiffen beside him. Heavy footsteps were marching towards them.

"They're coming!" she whispered.

CHAPTER SEVEN

The islanders processed solemnly into the cave. Many carried flaming torches, the light making their shadows dance over the walls. The men chanted in low voices as they moved towards the pirates. They stopped and, holding the lights high, began to thump their spears on the ground, slowly at first and then faster and faster.

"I told you the islanders would punish us for waking the dragon," muttered Fernando. "We're going to be killed."

But at that moment, the men parted and women came forwards. They were carrying large bowls, and each one was piled high with food!

The leader banged his spear on the ground and pointed towards the bowls. The pirates stared at him and he banged his spear again.

"Fill bellies!" he commanded.

Ned peered at the bowl nearest him. "Smells good," he said. He picked up a hunk of meat to bite into it.

"No!" Sam grabbed his arm. "It could be poisoned."

Ned looked longingly at the meat. "Do you think so?" he sighed. "I'm that hungry ..."

Sam's stomach rumbled. "Me too, but it could be our last meal."

"Food good," said one of the islanders, putting some into his mouth. He chewed and swallowed and then held a bowl out to the captives. "Food safe."

The pirates fell on the feast.

"It tastes wonderful," said Charlie, biting into a crusty chunk of bread.

"Peter could learn a lot from these people," mumbled Ben with his mouth full.

"Maybe they don't mean us any harm," said Sam. "If they don't see strangers very often, they've probably just forgotten their manners." He fed Crow a sliver of papaya.

Ned chuckled. "There was me thinking they'd be feeding us to the dragon and it turns out they're just feeding *us*."

Ben tucked into some fish. "And after this feast, perhaps they'll let us go."

Fernando nodded eagerly, his earrings glinting in the torchlight.

The food-bearers withdrew to the cave entrance. They squatted and talked together in low voices in their strange language.

But Sam realised that someone hadn't gone with the others. A young girl stood in the shadows, holding a basket of fruit and watching Fernando intently. "You've got an admirer," Sam said, nudging him.

"She's probably never seen such a fine young pirate," said Fernando, tossing his long curls.

"It's not you she's watching," said Sam. "It's your earrings.

Look at her eyes moving when you turn your head."

Fernando unhooked one of the gold rings from his ear and held it out to the girl. She glanced at her people as if making sure no one was looking at her, then came slowly over. Setting her basket of fruit aside, she put out a finger and ran it over the metal hoop, her eyes full of wonder.

"I don't think she's seen anything like it," gasped Charlie. She looked at all the islanders. "I've just realised that none of these people wear jewellery."

"What's your name?" Fernando asked the girl. "I'm Fernando," he said slowly, pointing to himself. He pointed to Charlie and Sam and said their names too.

"Arendira," whispered the girl. She gazed again at the earring, sighed and pushed Fernando's hand away. Then she jumped up and ran to her leader.

"It looks as if she's asking him

something," said Charlie as Arendira pulled at the man's arm. She pointed at the pirates and then at the tunnel that led to the outside.

"I think she's suggesting that we should be set free," agreed Sam.

"But he doesn't like what she's saying," said Fernando, putting his earring back in his ear.

The chief was shouting and shaking his head fiercely. The pirates didn't understand his words but their meaning was clear.

"Not sure he thinks that's such a great idea," muttered Sam.

The women grabbed the bowls of food and the torches, and all the islanders made for the tunnel. The head man thrust his spear towards the pirates.

"Legs still!" he barked at them. Soon the cave was plunged into darkness again.

"Well, I'll go round the world in a hat!" came Ned's voice. "First they give us a feast, then they leave us in this miserable place! I can't make head nor tail of it!"

Sam realised that he could see a flickering light dancing on the wall of the cave.

"Someone's coming back!" he hissed.

"Get ready to fight," muttered Fernando. "If it's only one man then we can overcome him."

There was a quiet footfall and the next moment Arendira appeared, holding a small torch. She beckoned to them.

"What does the maid want?" asked Ned.

"Let's find out," said Sam. They followed her to the back of the cave.

Arendira held up her torch. "Chief say this is not for your eyes," she whispered, looking round fearfully as the flame lit up a painting on the smooth wall.

"It's all right," Sam assured her. "Everyone has gone."

"That looks very old," said Fernando,

peering at the bright colours. "It must have been painted by Arendira's ancestors."

"But why is she showing it to us?" asked Ben. "Their leader won't be too pleased if he finds out."

"I think she's trying to tell us something," said Charlie. "It looks like a sort of story. There's a dragon in it."

Arendira beckoned them close to the painting. It showed the towering mountain with a dragon asleep on its slope, lying on a huge pile of gleaming treasure. Figures stood around the sleeping monster. They wore clothes like the islanders and they were throwing rings and necklaces onto the golden heap.

"All your jewellery goes to the dragon?" Ben asked slowly.

"We not have jewellery." Arendira looked anxiously at Fernando's earrings. "Dragon will take it."

Fernando's hands flew to his ears. He took his earrings out and rammed them deep in his pocket.

"So that's why none of her people wear jewellery," whispered Charlie.

"Hey, look at that gold eye at the top of the picture," said Sam. "It's really bright. Wonder what that's for."

"There's another picture further along the wall," said Fernando, as Arendira moved the light along. "Look, in this one the islanders have made a home for the dragon." The painting showed a highly decorated building with a gaping stone dragon mouth. The building rose to a point just like the ancient Aztec pyramids he'd seen in books. It stood on the mountainside and formed the entrance to a network of tunnels that wove down to underground chambers. In the deepest cavern the dragon lay asleep on its treasure.

"And there's another gold eye," said

Charlie, pointing at the staring orb with its scaly lids.

They followed Arendira to a third picture. Here, a boat full of people wearing rich robes and ruffs round their necks had landed on the shore of the island. The pirates could see that these people were not islanders. In the mountain, the dragon had woken from its sleep, its eyes flaming red. A golden dragon eye glared out of this painting too.

"Look, strangers have come and they've woken the dragon!" said Sam. "Just like the islanders think we've done."

Arendira moved her candle to the next picture. "See." Her voice was hardly more than a whisper and she trembled as she spoke. Her torchlight fell on a terrible scene. The people from the boat were deep underground in the maze of tunnels. The bright gold eye symbol gleamed above their heads.

"Those folk look terrified!" whispered Ned.

As the light passed over the scene the pirates gasped in horror.

"They have good reason," replied Fernando. "They're staring death in the face!"

The dragon was standing over them, breathing fire!

Silently they moved on to the last painting. The dragon was now feasting on human remains.

"So that's our fate," whispered Charlie in

horror. "We're going to be taken to the temple, roasted in dragon fire and—"

"Served up for its dinner!" wailed Ben.

CHAPTER EIGHT

Deep in the mountain, the rumbling came again.

"Dragon angry!" said Arendira urgently. "You must escape from its house – yes? If you clever, dragon not eat you."

"But how do we escape?" asked Sam. "Is there a way out?"

"Yes, but we not know it," said Arendira. "Has been forgotten. Ancestors build dragon house many, many years ago. My people not go in. But ancestors knew the way."

Footsteps sounded along the passage. Arendira leapt away from the pictures, and beat her torch flame out on the floor. They heard her scurrying away in the dark.

"She was trying to help us," said Charlie. "If only she knew the way out like her ancestors did."

"She said 'If you clever . . .'," muttered Ben.

"I don't see how being clever will help us escape a fire-breathing volcano dragon," said Sam. "Having fireproof suits would be more useful!"

"What are you talking about?" asked Fernando.

"Take no notice of his rambling," said Charlie quickly. "They're probably something his mother told him about – as she's such a dragon expert."

"We're not going to be killed," said Ned. Sam could hear that he was trying to keep their spirits up. "We'll find our way out – and if we fail, Captain Blade is sure to have a plan to rescue us."

"But he doesn't know where we are," came Ben's doubtful voice. "And we're up against so many."

He stopped as the distant sound of a drum reached them. It grew louder, then torches suddenly flared at the cave entrance and a group of islanders came towards them, keeping time with the beat. They now wore dragon headdresses, with glaring

eyes and pointed teeth. Their chief led the way. He had a cloak of golden scales.

"Dragon wakers, rise!" ordered the chief with a wave of his hand.

The five pirates got to their feet.

"Let's go down fighting!" muttered Ned.

As their captors made to seize them, Fernando let out an ear-piercing battle cry and they darted forward to attack. For a moment the islanders were taken by surprise.

Then the leader barked out a command and the men fell on the pirates. They outnumbered their captives by ten to one.

The *Sea Wolf* party was not going quietly. Ned laid about him with his huge fists. Ben whirled round, kicking out hard, and Fernando punched and shoved. Crow flapped his wings in their captors' faces while Sam tried to knock their feet from under them.

He saw Charlie creeping unseen along the wall. *Go, Charlie*, he thought to himself. *If she can get free, she'll bring the others back to help us.* Arms flailing like a windmill, he yelled at the top of his voice, hoping to draw attention away from her escape. As he knocked headdresses flying, he caught sight of her disappearing down the tunnel.

Soon the islanders had overpowered Sam and the others. Crow flew back down onto Sam's shoulder, grinding his beak angrily.

"Where's Charlie?" Ned whispered anxiously in Sam's ear.

"She got away!" Sam whispered back.

But at that moment a writhing prisoner was hauled back into the cave, scratching and biting.

"Good try, Charlie," called Fernando, as

the fierce girl pirate was bundled back among them.

"I nearly made it!" she panted, still struggling against the strong arms that held her.

"Tongue still!" snapped the chief. "Dragon ready. You come now."

"Wait!" exclaimed Ned. "I'm the biggest. Throw me to your dragon. That'll fill his belly. Let the others go."

"Never!" boomed the chief. "Dragon wants all." He turned and strode out of the cave. The men followed, marching to the drumbeat, forcing the pirates to walk with them along the tunnel.

"You were going to sacrifice yourself for the rest of us, Ned," Sam said in admiration as they were jostled along. "That was brave."

"Didn't work though, did it?" said Ned, shaking his head sadly. "Seems their dragon's got a big appetite."

The procession emerged from the tunnel into the cool night air. The mountain rumbled, making the ground shake again. The islanders began a low, slow chant with strange words that Sam didn't understand. He looked anxiously up at the volcano that towered over them. Fierce sparks were spewing from it and flames shot into the black sky. The sight was so terrifying that Sam was almost ready to believe there really was a dragon lurking inside. Dragon or erupting volcano, he certainly didn't want to be marching towards it.

Some of the women placed wreaths of dried flowers and leaves over the pirates' heads. The chief led the procession through the trees towards the fiery peak. The pirates stumbled on the rough ground but grasping hands dragged them to their feet. The islanders' chanting was almost drowned out by the sound of the rumbling volcano and the deadly hissing of the fire above.

At last a large clearing came into view. The pirates were thrust into the middle of it. The chief raised his hands and the chanting stopped. His people turned slowly to face a wall of stone. A huge carved dragon's mouth gaped hungrily in the middle of it. A feeling of dread came over Sam. This must be the dragon's house. It was exactly like the one in the wall painting. The stepped pyramid rose above them, black against the darkening sky. One side of the pyramid was the mountain itself.

And though Sam knew there was no volcano dragon inside the mountain, there was still something deadly down there, waiting for them.

CHAPTER NINE

The leader of the islanders held out his hands to the stone dragon mouth and chanted more strange words under his breath.

"What is he saying?" whispered Charlie.

"I don't know," Sam whispered back. "But I can guess. It's probably 'Here's dinner'."

Charlie gulped. "How are we going to get out of this one?" she murmured.

Sam squeezed her hand. "There's got to be a way," he said in a low voice. "If only we can think of it."

He stared at the temple with its hideous, gaping mouth. It was amazing, just like the one in *Aztec Adventure*, a computer game he had at home. Everyone at school was playing it. You had to work out how to open the door of each level so you could carry on with your quest to find the priceless golden pineapple.

The chief gave an order and his men marched Sam and his shipmates towards the temple entrance. They were pushed inside the stone mouth.

"Dragon eat," cried the leader. "Dragon sleep."

"Dragon eat. Dragon sleep," chanted the islanders.

The words filled Sam with an icy feeling.

As the heavy doors ground slowly shut, Sam saw, in the last flickers of the

torchlight, that they were in a large
stone chamber. He just caught sight of a

shiny black floor before they were
plunged into total darkness. He heard a
rustling as his friends threw down their
wreaths. He wrenched his loose and
dropped it, glad to be rid of the
scratchy dead leaves.

"Time for bed!" Crow croaked in a low
squawk.

The floor trembled and the sound of the
rumbling mountain echoed around them.
The air grew hotter.

"The volcano dragon's getting closer,"
came Ben's frightened voice.

"Then we have to find a way out!"
declared Sam. "But it's too dark to see
anything."

"I'll use my candle stub," said Fernando,
"now that there's no one to take it from
us." Sam heard him ferreting about. "But
how will I light it?"

"There's one or two stones underfoot
that might make a spark," came Ned's

voice, "and we'll use those dead leaves they presented us with as a taper. They'll catch fire easily and we can light your candle from that."

Sam saw the flash of stone on stone and a small flame flickered as the dead leaves caught fire. Fernando quickly brought his candle over to the flame and it sputtered into life, showing their circle of pale faces.

Ned and Ben ran to the big stone doors to try and prise them open, but they wouldn't budge.

Sam forced himself to think. "Remember those paintings in the cave," he said urgently.

"There were lots of chambers in the dragon's house, weren't there?"

"Linked by tunnels," agreed Fernando.

"Exactly!" exclaimed Sam in excitement. "And we're inside the dragon's house now, so there must be a tunnel somewhere that leads out of here. All we have to do is find it before the dragon arrives."

Everyone followed Fernando and his candle round the chamber, searching desperately for an escape route.

The hard shiny floor lay in swirly ridges that made it hard to walk. It was as if dark concrete had been poured from a mixer and then set before it could be smoothed out. Sam knew he'd seen something like it before but he couldn't think where.

"Look at these!" gasped Charlie. "They're horrible." She was standing by a huge wall mosaic showing monstrous fire-breathing dragons. The dragons' eyes caught the candlelight and shone with an evil red glow.

"I've found a way out!" called Ben suddenly. "Above our heads."

Fernando raised his candle to reveal a huge gaping hole in the ceiling.

"It's very black and charred," said Charlie. "It reminds me of a chimney."

"Looks like it goes high inside the mountain," said Ned. "I can see an orange glow up there. It'll be a hard climb but it's worth trying."

Despite the heat in the chamber Sam suddenly felt as if he'd been plunged into icy water. He looked at the floor. He now recognised it from pictures he'd seen on the internet. This was what the ground looked like when volcanic lava had flowed over it and then hardened. And he knew exactly what the distant orange glow was — more lava! He needed to warn his friends in a way they'd understand.

"That glow is deadly dragon fire," he told them. "Any minute now a load of the stuff is going to pour down on top of us! We can't escape that way!"

"Dragon fire!" screeched Crow, flapping his wings in alarm.

"I don't want to meet that dragon," cried Ned.

"Don't worry," said Sam, grimly. "We'll be cooked to death long before it turns up."

The pirates ran round the walls, desperate to escape the chamber.

"It's getting hotter," said Charlie in a small voice. "We're running out of time . . . Hey, what's this?" She ran her hand over one of the mosaics. "Hold the candle up here, Fernando. Yes, I thought so. All the other dragons' eyes have been painted in red, but this one is a sort of golden colour."

"So what?" said Fernando impatiently.

"We're about to be fried and you want to talk about art!"

"Hang on," said Sam. "This could be important. Remember those golden eyes in the cave paintings?"

"The ones that stared at us from every picture?" asked Ned.

Sam nodded. "They could be a sort of key."

"It doesn't look much like a key," said Fernando, examining it. "It wouldn't open any lock that I know."

"True," admitted Sam. "But I still think it might open something for us." He peered closely. The golden eye seemed to stick out from the mosaic. He tried to push it. Nothing happened.

"Look at the chimney!" cried Charlie. Bright orange lava was dripping through the hole in the ceiling.

Within seconds it was bubbling down the wall and creeping across the floor towards them. A stench like rotten eggs filled the air. Sam had read about molten lava smelling like that, but he had never imagined he'd be smelling it for real.

"It's the dragon fire!" cried Ben.

Chapter Ten

In desperation Sam pushed the eye again – harder this time. Now he felt it move. He could hear the lava hissing its way towards them. They were running out of time! He slammed both hands onto the eye.

There was a deep grinding sound and an opening appeared in the wall just above his head.

"Quick, everyone!" cried Ned, cupping

his hands. "I'll give all of you a leg up. You first, Charlie."

As soon as Ned had hoisted everyone into the opening, Ben and Fernando reached down and hauled him up to join them. Below them the fiery lava washed across the floor in surging waves.

"If we hadn't escaped," exclaimed Ned, "we'd have been burnt to a cinder!"

Charlie gave a wobbly grin. "Just like Peter's sausages! Well done, Sam. You saved us."

"But you found the eye in the first place, Charlie," replied Sam. "And I reckon that's the clue we needed. In the cave there was an eye in every painting — now we know why."

Fernando raised his candle to light up their surroundings. Long, winding steps led down into the dark.

"Come on," he said, leading the way. "Let's go."

The steps were carved out of the rock.

They twisted and turned deeper into the mountain.

At last another chamber opened out ahead of them. Fernando's flame lit up black walls covered in hideous paintings of pale human bones.

"Down among the dead men!" squawked Crow in Sam's ear.

"Not if I can help it," said Sam with a shudder.

Charlie inspected the stone floor and grinned with relief. "No sign of any dragon fire here, but it's just as hot."

A rasping, grinding noise echoed around them.

"The walls are moving!" cried Fernando.

"They're coming in towards us," gasped Sam. "Look for another golden eye, everyone, quick!"

"But there aren't any — golden or otherwise," Ned replied. "Skulls don't have eyes. They just have empty sockets."

Sam groaned. He'd been so sure that the eyes were the secret of the temple.

"We must hold the walls back!" declared Fernando, resting his candle on the floor. "It's the only thing to do if we're going to survive this."

The five pirates thrust their shoulders against the sliding stones, but it was no use. Their feet slid helplessly across the ground.

Ned stood in the middle, stretched out his strong arms and braced himself. The

walls were so close now that he had his palms flat against each one. But the walls kept grinding closer.

"We'll be squashed as flat as seaweed!" cried Ben. His foot knocked into the candle. It rolled over and over, its flame flickering wildly.

Sam dived to pick it up as it came to rest on something sticking up from the floor. He found himself looking down at a tiny, scaly eye. It shone gold in the candlelight. Had he been right that the eyes were the key, after all? Quickly he pressed it, but the heavy stone walls kept coming. He pressed harder. The walls towered over their heads now. There must be another way. In desperation Sam grasped the eye and pulled.

There was a deafening screech and the walls stopped their deadly advance. Then they slowly began to move apart.

The pirates fell to the floor, exhausted.

"Well spotted, Sam!" gasped Charlie. "But there's still no escape route."

Clunk! In front of them a trap door suddenly sprang open in the floor.

"There it is!" said Sam, leaping to his feet.

Fernando retrieved the candle and shone it through the hole.

"There's a passageway underneath," he said, "but it's a bit of a drop. Here goes . . ."

Before anyone could stop him, Fernando disappeared. There was a thud and then silence. The others looked at each other in alarm.

"What are you waiting for?" came his cheery voice. "The passage leads to another chamber."

Soon they were all standing in a high vaulted cavern. The walls were bare and battered, but the floor was covered in richly decorated flagstones. The torchlight caught the glint of gold. Every stone slab showed brightly painted dragons, curled up asleep. Not one had its eyes open, but Sam knew that there would be a golden eye somewhere for them to find.

"This floor's hot," said Charlie, skipping from foot to foot.

Suddenly Sam felt the flagstone beneath him begin to move. He leapt to join Fernando as the stone lowered itself and slid away with a clunk, leaving a gaping hole. Charlie's stone disappeared next, then flagstones started sliding away all around them. The pirates struggled to keep their footing on the remaining pieces of floor, jumping for safety each time a slab vanished beneath them.

"It's getting even hotter," panted Sam, as searing heat rose into the chamber. He sniffed the air and his heart sank. "I can smell rotten eggs again."

"There's a good reason for that," replied Fernando grimly. "Look what's beneath us!"

The pirates gazed down through the holes, blinking hard to shut out the sudden fierce glare. Far below bubbled a seething pool of bright orange lava.

Sam tried to think straight. Every chamber had a way out. This one was no different. It was just a question of finding the key to their escape before the floor disappeared completely and they dropped to a terrible death. He scanned the walls frantically . . .

Then he saw it! A staring golden eye, away in a far corner, but it was so high up there was no hope of reaching it in time.

Slam! Ned's slab slid away.

"I think this is the end for us," muttered Ben, catching Ned by the arm and pulling him onto his flagstone. The two men stood, wobbling as they tried to balance on the tiny stone.

"Wait a minute," cried Charlie. "The
floor's not moving any more!"

She was right. The grinding had stopped
and the remaining flagstones were still in
place under their feet.

"And I've seen the next eye," said Sam,
full of sudden hope. "Over there in that
corner. It's very high up, but if we get over

to that flagstone underneath it and make a sort of human tower, I reckon we might be able to reach it."

"Let me at it!" cried Ned.

The pirates began to move across the chamber, jumping from slab to slab as if they were playing hopscotch. Sam and Fernando were still picking their way over the disappearing floor when the others reached the flagstone. Ned bent his knees to make the base of the tower. Ben climbed on to his back and had just reached a hand down to pull Charlie up when . . .

WHOOSH! Everyone jumped in alarm as a huge metal ball suddenly swung down on a chain from the ceiling. It was coming straight at Fernando.

CHAPTER ELEVEN

With lightning reactions Fernando ducked and the heavy ball slammed into the wall, raising a cloud of dust. At once another came flying through the air, swinging wildly on its chain. Soon the chamber was full of huge metal balls thudding into the walls.

Sam yelped as a ball swung at him,

glancing off his shoulder and making him wobble violently over the drop. Crow gave a terrified squawk and flew into the air, frantically flapping his wings. Feathers fluttered down into the seething lava where they were instantly curled to a crisp.

The ball flew up, bounced off the wall right next to the eye and came hurtling down past him again. Suddenly Sam saw his chance to reach the eye and leapt at the ball, clasping its chain. He felt himself slipping and pulled with all his strength to heave himself up so that he was sitting astride the ball.

"Hold tight!" he heard Charlie yell.

The ball swung towards the eye, but with Sam on board it began to spin. He couldn't tell where he was. Then suddenly the wall was approaching fast – too fast. And where was the eye? Sam couldn't see

 it. He stretched out his hand. For a moment he thought he was going to miss, but suddenly there it was staring at him, gleaming pale gold in the harsh glow of the lava. As the ball whacked the stone wall, Sam flung his outstretched palm at the eye and pushed it hard. It didn't move.

Think! He told himself as the ball swung away. *Pushed the first eye. Pulled the second. What will it be this time?*

The ball was already zooming back towards the eye. Sam reached out, grasped it and gave a twist.

He heard Fernando give a whoop of delight.

"Well done, lad!" cried Ned. "A doorway's opened!"

Sam clung on, spinning helplessly. The ball went on swinging, clanging into others. He caught glimpses of his friends using the slabs as stepping stones to leap towards a gap in the wall. If he was going to go with them there was only one thing for it – he'd have to jump for the exit! He could only see a couple of flagstones left there, making a small platform, and if he missed them he'd plummet to a sizzling death in the lava.

The next time the ball swung low, Sam let go. He landed with a thud on the platform but felt himself begin to topple backwards. His arms flailed but it was no good. He was going to be fried.

Someone grabbed the front of his jerkin. He looked down to see a strong hand clasping the worn leather. Ned had got him!

"Thanks," panted Sam as he was hauled to safety.

"You're a hero!" said Charlie.

"All in a day's work," said Sam dizzily. He stumbled through the little gap into a steaming hot passageway.

Crow plonked himself down on his shoulder and nibbled his ear. "Ahoy there, matey!" he chirped.

Ben groaned. "We're heading further down into the mountain. I wonder if we'll ever see the sea and sky again."

"We have no choice," said Fernando, grimly. He held up his candle but at that moment it spluttered and died. As it became dark around them, Sam realised there was a bright glow ahead.

"I would have said it was impossible, but I believe it's even hotter here," groaned Ben, the sweat streaming off his face. "I hope we're not heading straight for the dragon."

"The passage is getting wider!" cried

Charlie as they inched forwards. She pointed along the walls. "Look, it's opening up."

They soon found themselves on a narrow ledge that looked out over a sea of lava. In the centre was a raised platform and on it lay a gleaming mound of golden jewellery as tall as three men. The smell of the lava was almost overpowering, clutching at their throats and making their eyes water. Sam decided he never wanted to eat eggs again.

"Well, I'll be a herring in a hairnet!" exclaimed Ned, pointing at the gold. "That's a mighty haul."

"If this is the dragon's treasure," whispered Fernando, "then the dragon can't be far away."

A deep rumble shuddered through their bodies. The lava surged higher, forming huge bubbles that burst and sent sparks high into the air.

"Sounds like he's coming!" gasped Ben, looking round wildly at the bare rock. "Where's the next eye? There are no paintings or mosaics or anything."

The rumbling was getting stronger. Sam knew there had to be another way out, there just had to be, before the eruption killed them all.

He thought about level forty-five on *Aztec Adventure*. It had taken him ages to get through that one. He'd been searching for a tiny arrow and it had turned out that the whole floor was in the shape of an arrow. Perhaps he was thinking too small.

Sam scanned the treasure cave. The craggy rock walls glowed in the light of the lava, throwing up dark shadows. There were no flashes of gold anywhere, but as he stared, a shape gradually stood out from the rock. It was an eye – not a little one like the others, but a gigantic, glaring eye with a heavy lid – as big as the *Sea Wolf*'s hull. And round its rim was a thin line of gold.

Sam leapt up with excitement. "There's an eye – over there, high on the wall."

The others followed his gaze.

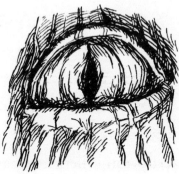

"That's just rock," said Charlie, narrowing her eyes. "How can you see a tiny little eye from here?"

"It's not tiny," said Sam. "It's huge." He wondered if he was imagining it. "Can't you see it? That dark bit? That's the pupil."

"I see what you mean," cried Fernando. "It's a massive dragon's eye."

But now Sam was worried. "We've got a problem," he said. "The other eyes were small. This one's so big, it will be impossible to move."

CHAPTER TWELVE

Crow took off from Sam's shoulder
and flapped up towards the massive
eye.

"Anyone would think he was trying to
help!" laughed Fernando.

They watched the parrot land on the
rocky eyelid. He cocked his head at the
dark pupil, gave a squawk and flew straight
at it.

"Crow!" yelled Sam as his feathered friend disappeared from sight.

"Down we go!" his screech echoed back to them.

"It must be a tunnel," gasped Ned. "Crow's found the way out of here!"

"Let's climb up after him," said Sam.

"Are you sure?" asked Ben. "One slip would be fatal."

"Aye," agreed Ned, looking down at the seething lava. "If you fell you'd be boiled alive before you could say 'dragon fire'."

"So we've got nothing to lose either way!" declared Fernando, getting to his feet. "I'm with you, Sam. I'll go first. I'm the better climber."

Sam knew he was right. Fernando had been swinging up and down ships' rigging all his life. They picked their way round the lava pool until the ledge gave out. The wall rose in front of them and they could see the eye far above. It looked a very long way off.

"Come, my friend," called Fernando. "Just imagine we're on the *Sea Wolf* making for the crow's nest."

Using spurs of rock as hand- and footholds, Fernando began to climb. Sam followed. As they got higher, the air grew even hotter. The handholds were so small that Sam found he was gripping with his fingertips. Fernando was almost under the eye now. He reached out a hand and grasped the bottom of the eyelid. But suddenly his feet missed their footing. He was dangling over the boiling lava.

His feet scrabbled to find a foothold as his fingers started slipping. Fernando was going to fall!

Sam quickly scrambled up until he was just below his friend.

"Put your feet on my shoulders," he panted, gripping tightly to the rock. He felt Fernando's foot come down on his head and braced himself to take his weight.

"Thanks," called Fernando. Sam could hear the wobble in his voice as he pulled himself over the lid of the giant eye and then reached down to help Sam up to join him.

Once they were both safe on the eyelid, Fernando held up his hand. "If ever there was a time for one of your high fives, this is it!" he said with a beaming smile. He whacked Sam's palm with gusto.

Rubbing his hand, Sam peered into the huge dark hole.

"Ned was right, it's another tunnel," he said. "It must lead somewhere or Crow would have come straight back." He turned and called to his friends in the cavern. "Fernando and I will see if there's a way out and let you know."

"Aye, aye," Ned called back.

"If only I had another candle," said Fernando. "It looks darker than Satan's soul. And suppose the volcano dragon's waiting at the end."

Sam felt a breeze on his face. "I can smell fresh air, but I'm not getting excited about that. This place has been full of deadly tricks and this could be another one."

He began to move forward on his hands and knees. The rock was very smooth and slippery. He tried to make out what lay ahead, but the dark was a thick blanket in front of his eyes.

"Perhaps we should try and make a torch to light our way," said Fernando.

"There's no time," replied Sam. "I'll just have to risk it. I'll take it slowly and— HELP!"

All of a sudden the floor seemed to disappear beneath him and he went hurtling downwards on the steepest slide he'd ever known. The tunnel twisted him this way and that in the pitch black. *It's like an underground flume,* he thought as he whooshed faster and faster on his belly. *But at least you know where you're going to end up on a flume!* He remembered what Fernando had said and imagined the open, drooling mouth of a mighty dragon waiting for him at the end of his ride. He closed his eyes.

Suddenly he felt himself flying through the air. There was an almighty splash as he hit water – cold, deep water. As Sam kicked to the surface he decided that this was not the inside of a fiery dragon. He shook the water out of his eyes. He'd been catapulted out of the volcano into a pool surrounded by rocks. Above him was the dark sky, full of twinkling stars. He'd found the way out! The mountain towered above him and he could just make out the opening of the tunnel in its side. Sparks were shooting high into the air from the volcano's peak. It was still erupting.

"Avast, me hearty!" came a familiar screech and Crow landed on his head.

With his parrot on board, Sam swam to the edge of the pool.

"Sam!" came Fernando's voice, echoing and strange. "Are you all right, Sam?"

"I'm fine," Sam shouted into the

tunnel. "I've escaped. Tell the others to come."

Sam hauled himself onto a rock and waited. He could imagine his shipmates scrambling up the wall towards the eye, Fernando helping to haul them to safety. He hoped they'd be able to make the treacherous climb.

Ben suddenly shot out of the rock flume, landed with a splash in front of Sam and disappeared under the surface. The water churned and he popped up, shaking his long wet hair out of his eyes.

"Get ready for a tidal wave," he chuckled. "Ned's right behind."

He thrashed to the side as the huge figure of Ned Wainwright hurtled into view, arms and legs flailing.

"Leave some water in the pool," laughed Sam as the bosun sent a wave slopping over the rocks.

"Only two to go," said Ben, pulling himself out to sit by Sam. "Then we'll find the crew and get off this infernal island."

Ned climbed out and the three pirates waited for Fernando and Charlie to appear. Time passed and there was no sound from inside the tunnel.

Something must have happened, thought Sam. *Surely they should be coming out now?*

Suddenly, a tremendous explosion split the air. Flames burst from the top of the volcano, lighting the night sky, and a fierce river of lava poured down the mountainside. The rock pool was directly in its path.

"Where are they?" muttered Ned. "There's not much time before that gets here."

At last they heard distant voices echoing down the tunnel.

"I can't do it, Fernando!" Charlie sounded terrified. "You'll have to go without me. I can't swim."

"You have to go!" came Fernando's reply. "You don't want to be eaten by the dragon, do you?"

"No, but I'm too scared! Nothing on this earth will make me slide down into a—Ahhhhhh!"

Charlie's words ended in a long scream. Sam, Ben and Ned stared at each other in horror.

"Has the beast got her?" breathed Ben.

Chapter Thirteen

The screaming was growing louder. The three pirates scrambled up the rocks to try to get to the tunnel entrance. But before they could reach it, Charlie flew past them, shrieking at the top of her voice. She hit the water with a resounding splash. Sam dived in and hauled her, kicking and spluttering, onto the rocks.

"Fernando pushed me!" she complained.

There was an almighty whoop and
Fernando somersaulted gracefully into the
pool.

"Come on!" yelled Sam as his friend's
head broke the surface. "We have to leave."
The lava was so near he could hear it
popping and bubbling.

The five pirates clambered over the rocks
away from the pool, with Crow flapping
anxiously over their heads. A loud hiss
behind them made Sam look over his
shoulder. The lava was streaming down
into the pool, boiling the water as it
poured in. Thick clouds of steam rose into
the air.

Ned wiped his forehead. "We were
nearly as stewed as Peter's barnacles."

"We're still going to
be stewed if we don't
get away from
here," said Ben.
"Follow me."

They raced over the rocks and down to the sand.

"There's the *Sea Wolf*!" shouted Fernando.

"And Captain Blade and the others!" exclaimed Charlie.

The crew had got the *Sea Wolf* upright and now she was floating in the shallows. As Sam and his friends ran up they saw Harry Hopp leading a band of men to the captain on the beach.

"Still no sign of them, Captain," they heard him say. "Do you think the volcano dragon's got them? It sounds mighty angry."

"What a terrible death," said Peter, staring mournfully down at his ladle.

"We're not giving up yet," declared Captain Blade. "Even though the *Sea Wolf* is repaired, we'll not set sail without our missing crew."

"And you have no need," boomed Ned. "We're back, safe and sound!"

The pirates turned at his voice and gave

a rousing cheer. The five friends were welcomed with pats on the back and swigs of rum. Sam only pretended to take a gulp of the horrible liquid as the bottle reached him. Crow flapped round their heads in excitement.

"By the tides, we spent all night searching the forest," said Captain Blade, shaking their hands in turn. "Where have you been?"

Sam quickly explained what had happened. The pirates' eyes grew wide as he told his tale.

"Shiver me timbers!" gasped Harry Hopp. "So you were nearly boiled up in dragon fire!"

"No dragon's going to outwit my brave crew!" exclaimed Captain Blade.

"Not while we've got a Silver on board," said Ned, giving Sam a friendly punch.

"Yo ho ho!" squawked Crow, swooping down and making the captain duck.

"And Crow did his bit," said Charlie, as the captain flapped the parrot away with his hat.

There was a terrifying cry and suddenly the crew found themselves surrounded by island warriors, waving and pointing their spears angrily.

"Dragon still hungry!" chanted the chief. "Five not enough. Dragon want more!"

The pirates' hands flew to their cutlasses. The islanders faced the crew, eyes blazing.

"We can take 'em," muttered Harry Hopp.

"Stop!" cried Sam, pushing to the front. "They don't understand."

The chief gave a cry of amazement. "You alive? You find way out?" he gasped.

"That's right," said Sam. "I had a word with the dragon."

"You speak to dragon?"

Sam nodded. "Your dragon is tired of eating people. He told us so himself."

"Did he?" said Ned, puzzled.

"I never heard him," added Ben.

"Yes you did." Charlie fixed them with a glare. "Remember?"

A slow smile spread over Ned's face as he realised that he had to play along with the story. "Oh, yes, that's right. Of course I do. We had a good old chat."

"Indeed," agreed Ben, nodding vigorously. "Friendly fellow, that dragon, when you get to know him."

"But dragon angry!" The chief pointed at the volcano. He still looked doubtful.

"He's sorry about that," said Sam. "He has a bad temper. You just need to stay out of his way when he gets like this."

He pointed up at the peak where the flow of lava had become a narrow stream. "See, he's not as cross as before."

The islanders began to talk among themselves, casting furtive looks at the pirates.

Then the chief held up his hands for silence.

"Anyone who finds way out of temple is hero," he announced. "That is word of our ancestors."

Captain Blade swept off his hat in a bow. "Thank you for your kind words," he said, "but now we must be off."

"Just remember to stay away from the dragon until he's calmed down," said Sam.

The islanders shouldered their spears and left the beach — except for one small figure who stood shyly at the edge of the sand.

"That's Arendira," said Fernando. "We must thank her. I'll give her one of my earrings."

"No," said Charlie. "She'll think the dragon will want it."

"Then I'll make her a bracelet that no dragon would want." Fernando quickly plaited some seaweed into a circle, threading shells into the weave.

Arendira beamed with delight as he handed it to her.

"Thank you for showing us the paintings," he said. "We would never have escaped otherwise."

"Dragon heroes always welcome here," she told him.

She slipped her bracelet on and then stood on tiptoes to kiss him on the cheek. Fernando went bright red and didn't say another word until the ship was under full sail.

The *Sea Wolf* cut swiftly through the waves. The crew were happy to be underway and the riggers sang a cheerful shanty as they pulled on the sheets to trim the sails.

"Stap me vitals, you can feel the difference in the ship after the careening," called Harry Hopp, who had the wheel. "She's handling like a new vessel."

"Aye," agreed the captain. "You'd think the dragon was after us, she's going so well."

Sam leant against the poop deck rail with Charlie. Crow sat on his shoulder, nibbling at an apple. They watched Dragon Island fade into the distance. The volcano was quiet again and all that could

be seen was a small, swirling cloud of
steam above the peak. The cloud began to
change shape. For an instant it formed a
long snout and wide pointy wings.

Sam gasped and grabbed Charlie's arm.
"Look at that!"

"Well, you did want to see a dragon,"
laughed Charlie. The shape billowed and
changed. "Though it looks more like a
tortoise now."

"Barnacle stew!" came a cry and Peter

stomped out of the galley, carrying a black cauldron. He plonked it down on the deck. "Time for a feast!"

"Faugh!" gasped Charlie, wafting the air in front of her nose. "That smells worse than the volcano, but we'll hurt Peter's feelings if we don't have some."

"It'll hurt my stomach if I do," muttered Sam with a grin.

Sam felt his fingers and toes tingle. He knew what that meant – his magic coin was about to whisk him back to the future. He dived behind a barrel so that no one else would see him go. "Saved by the doubloon!" he called to Charlie.

His words echoed round him as he was sucked up into the dark whirlwind and deposited back on his bedroom floor with a thump.

The rain still battered at the window but Sam didn't mind. After all, he'd just been deep inside an erupting volcano – and played *Aztec Adventure* for real!

He wished he could tell his friends at school, but undercover pirates never reveal their secrets!

CREW MANIFEST

Sinbad

Crow

Thomas Blade
Captain

Peter Craddock
Ship's Cook

Fernando
Rigger

Don't miss the next exciting adventure in the
Sam Silver: Undercover Pirate series

THE DOUBLE-CROSS

Available now!
Read on for a special preview
of the first chapter.

CHAPTER ONE

Sam Silver sat in his bedroom chewing his pencil. He was supposed to be doing a school project. Everyone in the class had to design a shield to show something interesting about their family. And it had to be ready tomorrow.

Sam was stuck. His mum and dad ran The Jolly Cod, the only fish and chip shop in Backwater Bay, and they all lived in the flat above. So Sam had drawn a bit of battered haddock and a bag of chips on his coat of arms, but he didn't think his teacher would be very impressed.

He gazed round his room, desperately trying to dream up something really amazing about his family. His eyes fell upon the old bottle he'd discovered on the beach. Inside he'd found a dirty old gold coin sent to him by a pirate ancestor called Joseph Silver. When he'd tried to clean it, the doubloon had whisked him back in time to the *Sea Wolf*, a pirate ship in the Caribbean. He'd joined Captain Blade's crew and now, whenever he rubbed the coin, he zoomed back to 1706 ready for another adventure.

Sam leapt to his feet. Of course! He knew exactly what he was going to draw on his shield – the *Sea Wolf*.

Then he had an even better idea. He'd pop off to see his pirate friends right now. After all, he wanted to get his drawing of the ship perfect on his shield – and he couldn't possibly do that without going back and seeing her again. And no one would know he'd gone. Sam could keep his time travels a secret because no time ever passed in the present while he was being a bold buccaneer.

Sam rifled through the untidy pile of clothes on his bedroom floor. At the bottom of the heap were the tatty old jeans and T-shirt that he always wore for his pirate adventures. He pulled them on, tied his trainer laces and tipped the coin out of its bottle. It gleamed invitingly in his hand. He couldn't wait. Fizzing with excitement, like a bottle of lemonade that had been given a good shake, Sam spat on the coin and rubbed it on his sleeve. His project, his pile of clothes and his bedroom furniture all whirled past him in a blur. He clamped his fingers round the doubloon and shut his eyes, feeling as if he was being sucked into a giant vacuum cleaner.

He landed with a bump on a wooden floor and opened his eyes. He was back in the storeroom of the *Sea Wolf*. Up on deck all his friends would be hard at work. He couldn't wait to see them. As usual, Sam's friend Charlie had put his pirate clothes on a barrel ready for him. Charlie, who'd joined the crew on the run from her evil stepfather, was the only one who knew he was a time traveller. The others believed that he just slipped off home now and again to see his mother. And as all pirates loved their mums, this was all right by them.

Sam quickly pulled on his jerkin, tied his kerchief round his neck and stuck his spyglass in his belt. He flung open the storeroom door ready to leap up the steps to the main deck when something stopped him in his tracks. The only sound that reached him was the lapping of the waves against the hull. Why couldn't he hear the sails being hauled or shipmates shouting to each other and singing sea shanties? Something was wrong.

His heart in his mouth, Sam crept slowly up the staircase. He heard a deep laugh from the deck. But it wasn't one of the crew. It was an evil laugh that chilled Sam to the bone. He edged up a little until his eyes were level with the deck.

He gulped in horror. Captain Blade and the crew had been herded together against the port rail, and a bunch of cut-throat pirates were threatening them with cutlasses. Sam's friend Fernando was looking pale under his wild, curly hair, and Charlie was clinging to his arm for support. Ben Hudson, the quartermaster, was crouched on the deck, his head in his hands, and even big cheerful Ned Wainwright looked as if he was going to be sick.

Lording it over them from the rail of the deck above was a tall figure. Sam recognised that hard, cruel face with the eye patch and the grizzled beard. It was Blackheart, the nastiest pirate in the Caribbean. Sam felt as if someone had stabbed a knife into his heart. Captain Blade's mortal enemy had captured the *Sea Wolf* and taken the whole crew prisoner.

Sam knew his crew were the bravest pirates ever to sail the Seven Seas, yet here

they were, pale as ghosts, bent double and cowering in fright. And bold Captain Blade, who was frightened of no man, was almost on his knees. Was he pleading with Blackheart?

Sam rubbed his eyes and looked again at the crew. Now he could see that they were all holding their stomachs. He could hear groaning. They weren't frightened – they were in pain! What had Blackheart done to them?

Sam tiptoed back down the steps. He had to make a plan to rescue his crew. But at that moment something sharp seized his shoulder in a vice-like grip.